PUFFIN BOOKS

UK | USA | Canada | Ireland | Australia
India | New Zealand | South Africa

Puffin Books is part of the Penguin Random House group of companies
whose addresses can be found at global.penguinrandomhouse.com.

www.penguin.co.uk
www.puffin.co.uk
www.ladybird.co.uk

Penguin
Random House
UK

First published 2017
001

Written by Rebecca Lewis-Oakes
With thanks to Liss Norton
Illustrated by Helen Smith
Cover illustration by Faye Yong
Text and illustrations copyright © Arklu Limited, 2017
© 2012 Arklu Limited. *Lottie* is a trademark of Arklu Limited.
All rights reserved.

Printed in Great Britain by Clays Ltd, St Ives plc

A CIP catalogue record for this book is available from the British Library

ISBN: 978–0–141–37908–1

All correspondence to:
Puffin Books
Penguin Random House Children's
80 Strand, London WC2R 0RL

Lottie

Lottie Braves a Storm

LUCIE BRAVEHEART

PUFFIN

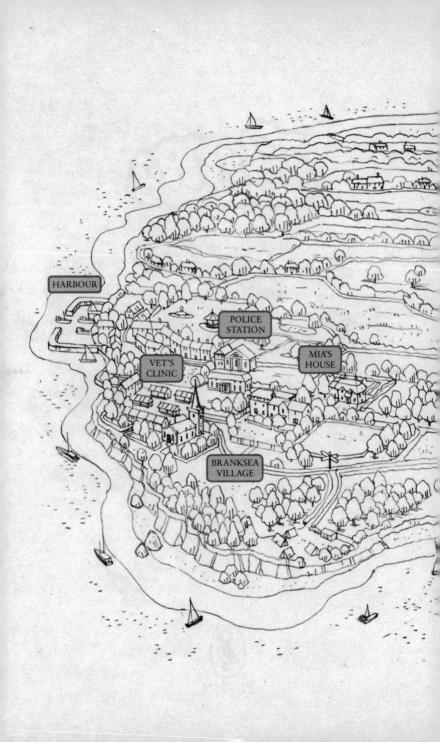

HARBOUR

POLICE
STATION

VET'S
CLINIC

MIA'S
HOUSE

BRANKSEA
VILLAGE

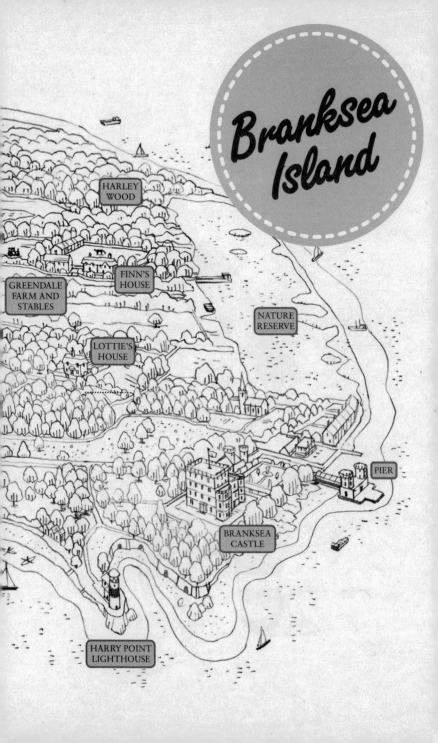

Branksea Island

HARLEY WOOD

FINN'S HOUSE

GREENDALE FARM AND STABLES

LOTTIE'S HOUSE

NATURE RESERVE

PIER

BRANKSEA CASTLE

HARRY POINT LIGHTHOUSE

Contents

Chapter One
Aunt Matilda's Bells

Tinkly tinkly tinkle . . . 'RUFF!'

Lottie giggled as her puppy, Biscuit, barked and ran in circles round the garden. Lottie was jingling a loop of tiny brass bells in front of him, and the tinkling sound made him especially playful!

Lottie had found the bells in

her Great Aunt Matilda's suitcase in the attic. Great Aunt Matilda – Gam for short – had been an explorer, and she had left all sorts of treasures in her suitcase. Lottie had read about the bells in Gam's notebook.

TRIP TO INDIA - A LUCKY BREAKDOWN

My motorbike broke down near a riverside village. Before I could find help, I heard a cry. I ran to the riverbank and saw a boy stuck deep in the mud by the water. I stepped on to the mud but my foot started to sink! So I grabbed some branches from a nearby bush and laid them over the mud to spread my weight. It would be no use for us both to get stuck!

I lay on the branches, wriggled over to the boy and pulled him out. We slid back to the shore and he helped me push my motorbike to the village. What a lucky breakdown!

I wouldn't have heard the boy's cries if my engine had been running. His parents gave me some beautiful ghungroo bells as a thank-you gift. Dancers wear ghungroo bells on their ankles, and they make a lovely tinkling sound!

Lottie jingled the lucky bells happily.

'RUFF! RUFF!'

As Lottie turned towards Biscuit, she spotted a flash of white in the bushes. 'What was that?'

She jingled the bells again

and saw another flash of white. Shushing Biscuit, she crept up to the bush.

Tinkly tinkle!

A bright white furball leaped out at Lottie. She just managed to catch it.

'Miaow,' purred the furball. It was a cat! It must have liked the sound of the bells.

'Hello, kitty,' said Lottie. 'Are you lost?' She looked in the cat's deep fur and found a collar. Its tag read 'PANDORA'.

'Lottie?' called Grandma from the back door. She was looking after Lottie while her parents helped her little sister, Sophia, at the Science Fair.

Lottie ran inside with the cat. 'Look what I found!' she said.

'My goodness!' exclaimed Grandma. 'A cat!'

'Can we take it to Cassie the vet? She might know if someone has lost their kitty.'

'Good idea,' said Grandma. 'Let's go.'

They put the cat in Biscuit's travel basket. Biscuit lay down with his head on his paws, looking sad about being left behind.

'We'll be home soon, Biscuit,' said Lottie. 'Don't worry!'

Lottie and Grandma arrived at the vet's just in time – Cassie was about to lock the door.

'Hello, Lottie,' said Cassie. 'Is Biscuit all right? I'm just closing up to do my farm rounds.'

'Biscuit's fine, thanks.' Lottie opened the travel cage. 'But I found a cat! Its name is Pandora. Has anyone reported a missing cat?'

'Not to me,' said Cassie. 'But well done for bringing it here. I'm in a rush now, and the cat doesn't seem unhappy, so let's put it in the cattery and I'll check on it first thing tomorrow.'

Lottie breathed a sigh of relief. The cat would be safe tonight. But now Lottie had a mystery to solve. Where had the beautiful cat come from?

Chapter Two
The Mystery Cat

The next day was cloudy. The weather forecast said a big storm was coming to Branksea Island. Lottie put on her coat and fetched Biscuit's lead.

'Time to crack the case of the mystery cat!' she told him.

It was lucky that Lottie's two best friends, Mia and Finn,

were coming over later for a pizza party. Together, they were the Branksea Adventurers' Club, and they had already solved one mystery on Branksea Island! Mia and Finn would help Lottie find the cat's owner.

The bell rang as Lottie and Biscuit entered the vet's surgery.

'Hello, Lottie! Is Biscuit all right?' asked Jill, the receptionist.

'He's fine, thanks! We've

come to see the cat we found.
Is it OK?' replied Lottie.

Jill smiled. 'Ah, it was you
who found it! Cassie hasn't
been in yet – she went straight
to Greendale Farm to check on
the sheep. But I'm sure she
won't mind if you have a look.'

Lottie let Biscuit out into the
vet's surgery garden then went
into the cattery to see Pandora.

Just as she was reaching in to
stroke the cat, Biscuit let out a
low growl from outside.

'Biscuit! Don't be jealous,' said Lottie, popping out to give him a quick cuddle.

'Lottie,' called Jill. 'I need to run out to buy sandbags to protect us from the storm. Would you take any messages for me, please?'

'Of course!' called Lottie, running back into the reception. She sat in Jill's chair and spun round in it, giggling when it made her dizzy.

Brrring, brrring! Brrring, brrring!

The phone on the desk was ringing. Lottie picked up.

'Branksea Veterinary Surgery,
how may I help you?' she said,
in her best grown-up voice.

The lady's voice on the
other end sounded upset. 'Oh,
hello. Please help me. I've lost

my cat and don't know how to find her!'

'What does the cat look like?' asked Lottie.

'She's beautiful, with fluffy white fur and blue eyes. She's called Pandora. I miss her so much!' said the lady.

Lottie sat up straighter. This solved the mystery of the lost cat! 'We've found a white cat called Pandora,' she said. 'Can you come to see her?'

The lady sighed gratefully.

'That must be her! But we can't come to collect her today because of the storm. We have a holiday cottage on Branksea Island, but we had to rush back to the mainland before the sea got too rough. Pandora escaped from her cage just before we left. Please keep her safe until we get there!'

'I promise,' said Lottie. She put down the phone and smiled. It was fun answering the phone like a grown-up!

Lottie went back into the cattery.

'Pandora, we've found your –' Lottie stopped in the doorway and gasped.

The door to Pandora's cage was open. She was nowhere to be seen!

'I forgot to close the back door, too!' Lottie whispered, holding her hands to her mouth. 'Biscuit, we've got to find Pandora – and fast!'

Chapter Three
The Search Begins

Lottie had just closed Pandora's cage and the back door when Jill got back.

'Thanks for your help, Lottie!' Jill said.

'You're welcome,' Lottie replied, fidgeting. She didn't want to tell Jill about Pandora. She was sure she could find the cat a second time before anyone noticed she was missing!

Lottie said goodbye to Jill and rushed out with Biscuit, heading for the park while she thought about what to do.

At the park, Lottie spotted her best friends on the swings.

'Mia! Finn!' she called, running over. 'You've got to help me!'

Finn laughed. 'Good morning to you, too, Lottie.'

Mia stopped swinging and turned to Lottie. Mia's cochlear implant helped her to hear but it was even better if she faced people when they were talking. 'What's happened?' she asked.

Lottie tried to catch her breath. She explained that she had found Pandora and taken her to the vet, but the cat had escaped. 'We have to find her before anyone notices she's missing!' Lottie said.

Mia frowned. 'Why didn't

you tell Jill, Lottie? I'm sure she
would have helped.'

'But it was my fault for
leaving the door open,' said
Lottie, looking down at her feet.
'And, anyway, if we can find
Pandora quickly then no one

needs to know. Will you help me?'

Mia looked unsure but Finn jumped in. 'Of course we will. We're the Branksea Adventurers' Club!' he said, and led the friends in their special club sign: a three-way high five. 'Where shall we look first?'

'Pandora's probably gone in search of food. Cats like fish and meat,' said Mia.

'You know a lot about cats,' said Finn.

Mia blushed. 'I'd love a cat for my birthday. Mum said I have to learn how to look after one first. So I've read a lot about cats at the library!'

'That's perfect. Well done, Mia!' said Lottie. 'Come on, let's get searching!'

The three friends looked everywhere for Pandora. They went to the fishmonger first, and then they tried the butcher. They even looked at Lucia's Pizza Palace, in case the cat liked Italian food, but they didn't find her there either.

Lottie slumped down on a bench across the road from the police station. 'What if we never find her?'

Mia pointed to the station. 'The police might be able to help.'

'I don't want to get into trouble,' said Lottie, scared.

'It's a good idea,' said Finn. 'Come on.'

Reluctantly, Lottie followed Finn and Mia into the station.

Finn had already started talking to Constable Potts at the front desk.

'Have I heard about any missing animals?' Constable Potts was saying. 'What's this about, Finn? Are animals disappearing from your farm?'

'No, I just, er . . .' Finn
stuttered.

Mia jumped in. 'The thing is,
there was a cat –'

Lottie cut her off. 'In a book
we read! About animal rustlers.

Are there animal rustlers on Branksea Island, Constable?'
Constable Potts sat down and opened his newspaper.

'I'm not messing about with stories from books. There are no missing animals reported on Branksea. Off you go.'

Back outside, Mia was a bit cross. 'Why didn't you let me finish asking about the cat?' she said to Lottie.

'I'm sorry. I just didn't want to get in trouble for leaving the cattery door open. We can find Pandora on our own!' Lottie replied.

Just then there was a loud

thunderclap and it started to rain.

Biscuit barked.

'Quick!' said Finn. 'Let's get back to Lottie's for our pizza party – the storm is on its way!'

Chapter Four
Braving the Storm

Later, Mia and Finn tucked into their pizza, but Lottie was so nervous she couldn't eat. What if they never found Pandora?

Outside, the storm was getting worse. Biscuit barked at the back door.

'He doesn't like thunder, does he?' said Mia.

'Ruff, ruff!' Biscuit replied.
The friends laughed.

Just then, Lottie's mum
came home from work and
opened the back door. Biscuit
darted outside!

'Biscuit, come back!' called Lottie. Not *another* runaway animal! She jumped up and followed the sound of his barking. He led her towards the bushes at the bottom of the garden.

The rain was falling hard now. The tree branches whipped in the wind and Lottie had to keep swiping her wet hair out of her eyes. Eventually, she found Biscuit standing next to a huge muddy puddle, still barking loudly.

'What's wrong, Biscuit?' she asked.

Mia and Finn ran up to Lottie, breathing hard.

'Is he stuck?' asked Finn.

'No, but I think he's trying to tell us something,' Lottie said.

'Look!' Mia pointed into the bushes beyond the puddle.

They could just make out something white through the rain and the leaves. 'Maybe it's Pandora!' Lottie said.

Lottie stepped forward but her wellies started sinking into the mud. Suddenly she remembered the story in Gam's notebook about how she had rescued the boy by the river in India.

'Quick,' Lottie said, 'grab some branches. They'll stop me from sinking.'

Mia and Finn collected branches and Lottie spread them over the muddy puddle. Carefully, she stepped on one. It held her weight. She walked slowly over the branches towards the bush and shifted the leaves aside.

To her surprise, it was not Pandora hiding there. It was four little white kittens!

Lottie gently picked up one of
the kittens, then stepped back
over the branches and handed the
kitten to Mia. Then she went
back for another one. Soon the
friends had rescued all four kittens.

Back in the kitchen, Lottie's
dad had towels ready for them.
'You three shouldn't go out in
the storm. It's cold – and
dangerous!' he said.

'I'm sorry, Dad,' said Lottie,
drying off two of the kittens.
'But look how white these kittens
are – they must be Pandora's!'

Lottie had told Mum and
Dad about finding Pandora, but
she hadn't mentioned losing her
again at the vet's. There was no
use telling everyone the cat was

missing when Lottie was sure
the Branksea Adventurers' Club
would find her any moment now!

Mia was helping Lottie's
sister, Sophia, to dry off the
other kittens. 'These kittens
look very young. They need
special milk,' Mia said. 'Should
we take them to the vet's?'

'We should, Mia,' said
Lottie's mum, 'but the road to
the vet's is closed because of a
tree that fell in the storm.'

'Let's take them to our farm,

then,' suggested Finn. 'My
parents have special milk formula
for feeding orphan lambs.'

'Good idea!' said Lottie's mum.
The kittens mewed quietly.

Mia looked worried. 'Cats don't usually leave their babies alone so soon,' she said. 'Maybe Pandora went off to hunt and got stuck somewhere? I hope she's OK.'

Lottie stood up. 'I'll go back out and look for her!'

'No, Lottie,' said Dad. 'Not in the storm.'

'And isn't Pandora at the vet's?' asked Mum.

Lottie stopped. She had been worried about getting into

trouble, but now she realized she was more worried about Pandora.

She took a deep breath and told the truth. 'I – I left the cattery door open by accident and Pandora escaped. We've been looking for her all day.' She hung her head.

Mum gasped.

'Lottie! Why didn't you say something?'

'Yes, Lottie. Pandora might have an electronic tag in her fur. Cassie could have tracked her by now,' said Dad, crossing his arms.

Lottie's lower lip trembled. 'I didn't think of that,' she said. 'I wanted to make things better by finding Pandora, but I've made everything worse. I'm sorry!' Lottie felt like she might cry.

Mum and Dad shared a look, then Dad gave Lottie a hug. 'Thank you for saying sorry. It's OK to ask for help, Lottie.

Better late than never.'

Lottie nodded and sniffed.

'If Pandora had the babies here, she can't be too far away,' said Mia. 'But the kittens need help now.'

'I'll let Cassie know about Pandora,' said Dad, picking up the phone. 'She'll have been out on call all day, with animals getting injured in the storm. You take the kittens to Finn's farm.'

Mum nodded and grabbed

her car keys. The friends gathered up the kittens, and everyone bundled into the car.

Chapter Five
Kittens in a Basket

Finn's parents jumped into action as soon as everyone arrived at the farm. His mum prepared a cosy basket for the kittens. His dad showed them how to use milk droppers, which were thin plastic tubes with rubber bulbs on the ends.

'You squeeze the bulb and a

little bit of special milk formula will drip out of the tube,' Finn's dad said, showing them.

Lottie held one kitten and carefully let a drop of milk fall into its mouth. The kitten licked its lips. 'It's working!' she said.

Once the kittens were fed,
Finn's mum put them in the
basket. 'Now we'll put them in
front of the country cooker,' she
said. 'They need to get warm!'

Mia didn't want to say
goodbye to the kittens, but
Finn's parents said they could
come and visit again tomorrow.

Back at home, Lottie lay in bed,
cuddling Biscuit. She was
worried about Pandora, and
she still felt guilty for not

telling the truth right away. She played with the ghungroo bells and wondered what Gam would have done in her place.

Tinkly tinkly tinkle.

Lottie sat bolt upright in bed. All of a sudden she knew exactly what Gam would do!

She pulled on her woolly hat and coat, fetched her torch and crept downstairs. Her mum and dad were watching TV in the living room, so they didn't hear her tiptoe into the kitchen and put on her wellies.

Lottie opened the back door. She felt bad that she was going to sneak out. But Dad had only

said not to go out into the
garden in the storm, and it had
stopped raining now . . .

    Quietly, Lottie stepped out
into the night.

Chapter Six
A Mew in the Darkness

The rain had stopped, and the garden looked silver in the moonlight.

'Let's find Pandora, Biscuit,' Lottie said. She turned on her torch and jingled the bells.

Tinkly tinkly tinkle.

'Miaow!'

Lottie heard a faint mew

from the bottom of the garden.
She hoped it was Pandora!

Biscuit followed Lottie as she
walked towards the mewing.
Every few steps she jingled the
bells again and the cat would

miaow in return. The sound was getting louder as she got closer.

Lottie reached the branches by the puddle where they had found the kittens, and she ducked under the hedge.

'Miaow! Miaow!'

The mews were much louder now. Lottie realized they were coming from above. She shone her torch and saw Pandora up a tree!

'Poor girl!' she said. 'Are you stuck?'

There was only one thing for it: Lottie had to climb the tree. She had climbed plenty of trees before and this one looked easy – to begin with. The low branches were nice and close together, but they got further apart up where Pandora was.

Lottie rested her torch on the tree trunk so it shone upward. She grabbed hold of the lowest branch and started to climb. She was just a few branches from Pandora when her foot slipped.

She almost fell!

Biscuit barked below her.

Trying to stay calm, Lottie held on tight to the branch above and found her footing again. 'I'm a brave Branksea Adventurer,' she reminded herself. 'I can do it!'

Slowly, Lottie climbed until she reached Pandora's branch. She gently took hold of Pandora with one hand. The beautiful white cat was soaking wet and mewing sadly.

'Your paw is hurt!' said Lottie.
'It's OK. I've got you now.'

Carefully, she put Pandora in
the front of her coat and made
her way back down to the ground.

Biscuit jumped up to greet them and barked. Pandora purred inside Lottie's coat.

Lottie ran back to the house with the torch, took off her wellies and locked the back door behind her. She put Pandora down next to Biscuit's bowls and filled them with water and dog food. Pandora ate it all up! And Biscuit didn't seem to mind sharing.

Lottie took both animals up to her bedroom. The three of them all snuggled up together. Within minutes they were fast asleep.

Chapter Seven
A Surprise for Mia

Lottie's parents were shocked when she came down to breakfast with Biscuit *and* Pandora.

'Where on earth did she come from?' asked Mum.

Lottie hugged the cat tightly. 'I found her last night . . . in a tree at the bottom of the garden.'

'Lottie!' Her dad frowned. 'We told you not to go out again.'

'I'm sorry. I was just so worried about Pandora! And look, her paw is hurt, and she was stuck up the tree!'

Mum shook her head. 'It's good that you found Pandora, but you should have asked us for help. Don't go out on your own at night again.'

'I'm really sorry. I won't do it again, I promise,' said Lottie.

Dad took Pandora from Lottie and gave the cat a hug. 'You'll have to apologize to Cassie for leaving the cattery door open, too. I'll ask her to come and check on Pandora now. Perhaps she can even bring the kittens.'

Lottie wolfed down her toast and got dressed in record time. She came downstairs again as Cassie was coming in with Finn and the kittens.

In their kitchen, Cassie bandaged Pandora's hurt paw.

'I was so rushed off my feet, I didn't have time to examine her when she came in. I would have noticed she was pregnant! Luckily the kittens are all fine and Pandora's paw will heal well, too,' Cassie said. 'Pandora's owners arrived on the ferry this morning. They're on their way here now.'

The doorbell rang and Mia and her mum arrived.

'Are the kittens here?' said Mia. 'I can't wait to see them again!'

Mia, Finn, Lottie and Sophia all had a last cuddle with the kittens.

The doorbell rang once more and a kind-looking elderly couple introduced themselves. 'I'm Camilla and this is George,' said the lady. 'Thank you so much for finding our precious Pandora!'

Pandora saw Camilla and purred happily. Lottie was thrilled that Pandora was back with her owners and that everyone was happy – but there was something she needed to say.

Lottie took a deep breath and turned to Cassie. 'I'm so sorry for leaving the door open and letting Pandora escape. I should have said something to Jill straight away. How can I make it up to you?'

Cassie looked serious.
'Thanks for saying sorry, Lottie.
If you really want to make it up
to us, you could come and help
clean the cattery next weekend.'

'Of course!' said Lottie.
'Thank you. I really am sorry.'
Then George said, 'Well,
Lottie, you did lose Pandora, but
you found her, too – twice!'

Now everyone laughed.

Lottie sighed with relief. She felt much better for telling the truth.

'I don't know what we'll do with the kittens,' George said. 'We didn't even know Pandora was expecting.'

'They're beautiful. I'll be sorry to see them go,' said Cassie.

'Me too,' said Lottie.

'Me three!' said Mia.

Camilla stroked a kitten. 'Would you all like to keep one,

as a thank-you for finding Pandora?'

Finn replied first. 'Thank you, but I have enough animals at home, on the farm.'

'And we already have a pet,' said Lottie, cuddling Biscuit.

Mia's eyes were open wide. 'Could I have one, please?' She turned to her mum. 'Can I?'

Mia's mum smiled. 'You can have one as an early birthday present,' she said.

Mia squealed in delight. Then she paused. 'I can't take it yet, though. Kittens need to stay with their mothers for at least eight weeks after they are born.'

Cassie was impressed. 'That's right, Mia! You obviously know how to look after cats.'

'We're coming back to the island in a couple of months,' said Camilla. 'Why don't we bring a kitten back for you then?'

Mia was so happy that she gave Camilla a hug. Then she hugged her mum. Then everyone was hugging, and cuddling the kittens, too!

When everyone had gone, Lottie carefully packed Gam's ghungroo bells back in the suitcase in the attic. Then she pulled out her Adventure Journal, and started to write.

The ghungroo bells led to a very exciting adventure. I found Pandora, lost her, and then found her again! But the bravest part was definitely when I had to own up to losing Pandora. That was even scarier than climbing the tree in the storm . . . I wonder what the next adventure will be for the Branksea Adventurers' Club!

Your story starts here . . .

If you love **BOOKS** and want to **DISCOVER** even more stories go to **www.puffin.co.uk**

- Amazing adventures, fantastic fiction and laugh-out-loud giggles
- Brilliant videos starring your favourite authors and characters
- Exciting competitions, news, activities, the Puffin blog and SO MUCH more . . .

Puffin is off to have a look!
www.puffin.co.uk